A Garden of Opposites

NANCY DAVIS

schwartz & wade books • new york

short

long

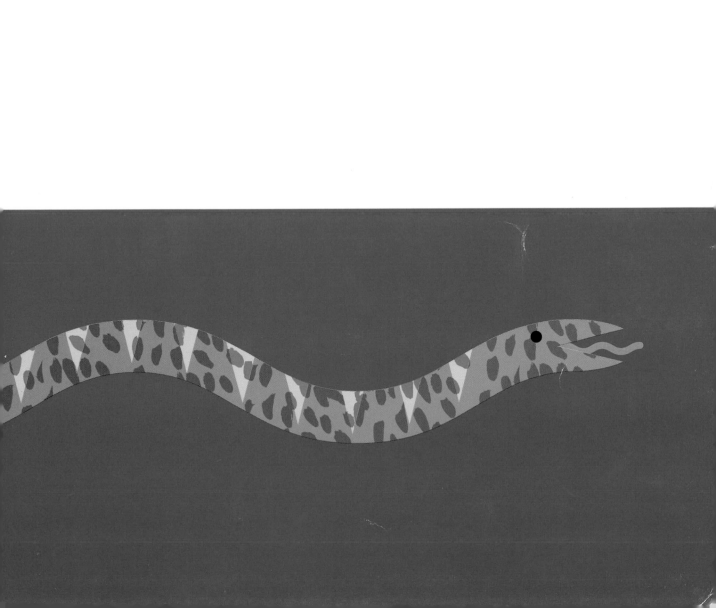

inside

outside

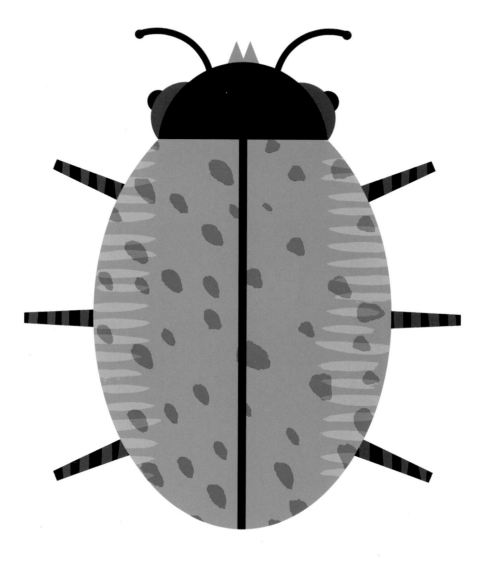

big

little

different

alike

plain

fancy

asleep

awake

dull

sharp

open

closed

in

out

See how many more opposites
you can find on this page!

To all those who find joy and wonder in a garden

Did you find all these opposites on the previous page? inside/outside (birdhouse), high/low (flying birds), above/below (bumblebees), many/few (apple trees near birdhouse), open/closed (flowers), fast/slow (bunny and snail), plain/fancy (butterflies), big/little (ladybug and beetle), long/short (snake and worm), upright/upside down (flowerpots), empty/full (strawberry boxes), different/alike (clovers), ripe/unripe (strawberries), tall/short (pea p